Get some FREE ebooks at
bit.ly/5freebooks

INGO BLUM

Where Is My Little Elephant?

Illustrated by Antonio Pahetti

planetOh concepts

4

Where is Daisy, my little elephant?

She is not in the china shop.

She is not in the circus.

There are many animals there. But no elephant!

Who else do you see?

Isn't today her birthday?

Perhaps she is with
her friends!

Is she at the ice rink?

No, there is no
elephant on that ice.

12 MONKEY

She is not at the zoo.

The animals are missing her.

14

She is not standing under the tree.

Is she hiding?

16

Is she making music?

No. Elephants cannot play a musical instrument.

She is not at school.

Is Daisy lazy?

She must
learn to read.

Look, there she is! Hooray!

Daisy is on a ship with her
friends, a lion
and a rhino.

We found her!

Daisy the Elephant

Coloring Book

More Reading and Coloring Fun

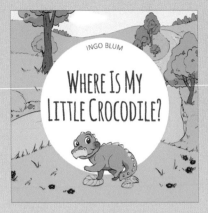

ISBN 978-1-982941-28-4

ISBN 978-1-982941-74-1

ISBN 978-1-982942-12-0

ISBN 978-3-947410-21-7

ISBN 978-3-947410-23-1

ISBN 978-3-947410-25-5

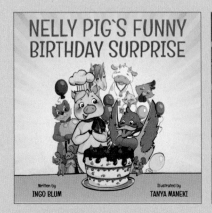

ISBN 978-1-983075-91-9

ISBN 978-1-982958-22-0

ISBN 978-3-947410-56-9

Thank You

Thank you for reading this little story. I hope you enjoyed it the same way I did while writing it. If you would like to know when my next book comes out, find more books I have written, and receive some occasional updates from me, just visit me on my website.

Do you find reader reviews helpful? If so, please spare a moment to help me by rating this book, so others will find it (and read it!), too. I always appreciate an honest review.

RATE NOW

Looking forward to your comments, reviews, and opinions.

About the Author

Ingo Blum is a German author and comedian. His journey to become a children's book author began during his day job. He has always enjoyed projects where he could create artwork for kids. He started writing stories to accompany these projects for fun, and with some encouragement from friends and family (and their kids!) he decided to share his stories with the world. Ingo works with international illustrators, with whom he constantly develops new concepts and stories.

About the Illustrator

Antonio Pahetti is a young artist with a lot of experience in children's illustration, who makes his illustrations with much love and a passion for details. His works are published in many countries. He lives in the Ukraine.

Made in the USA
Monee, IL
18 February 2022

91413543R00021